D0102789

HEART OF ICE

HEART OF ICE

BY THE COMTE DE CAYLUS
ADAPTED BY BENJAMIN APPEL
ILLUSTRATED BY J.K. LAMBERT

PANTHEON BOOKS

Published in the United States by Pantheon Books, a division of Random House, Inc., and simultaneously in Canada by Random House of Canada Limited, Toronto.

Library of Congress Cataloging in Publication Data
Appel, Benjamin, 1907–
Heart of ice.
Summary: Taken from his royal parents at his christening by one fairy to escape the vengeance of another, a prince, thinking he is a commoner, sets out to win the hand of a beautiful princess.
[*1. Fairy tales*] I. *Caylus, Anne Claude Philippe, comte de, 1692-1765.* II. *Lambert, James K.* III. *Title.*
PZ8.A677He [*Fic*] 76-4815
ISBN 0-394-83245-0
ISBN 0-394-93245-5 *lib. bdg.*

Designed by J. K. Lambert
Manufactured in the United States of America

For Francesca, Elena, and Adam Benjamin – B.A.

For my mother and father – J.K.L.

NCE UPON A TIME there lived a King and a Queen who were foolish beyond all telling. True, their kingdom had prospered, but only because the royal couple had sense enough to honor the Fairies and Enchanters whose goodwill was so necessary in those olden days. They loved to receive presents, and most important of all, they expected to be invited to the palace on every festive occasion.

The whole kingdom rejoiced when the Queen gave birth to a son, the heir to the throne, and the christening in pomp and ceremony was indeed the greatest of all great occasions. The Fairies and Enchanters, as was the custom, would be the guests of honor. The Queen immediately asked for pen and paper and began to write down the names of the Fairies and Enchanters. Whether good or bad, all had to be invited, none could be omitted.

The list was enormous. The foolish Queen forgot that it would take the King nearly as long to read it through as it had taken to write it out. No matter how fast the King could read, his tongue was no swifter than any other human being's. So, when the moment of the christening arrived, the excited Queen ran to the King and gave him the enormous list.

"Hurry, dear King," said she. "Make haste or our little Prince will regret this day!"

The King glanced at the endless columns of names on the first page. In order to summon the non-human guests from their castles he would have to read their names out one by one. From past experience he knew that the Fairies and Enchanters would appear instantly, once they were called, even if their castles were a thousand leagues from the palace. With a groan he began to recite the magic incantation:

"I conjure and summon you, Fairy Will-o-the-Wisp . . . I conjure and summon you, Enchanter Azarael . . . to honor me with a visit, and graciously bestow your gifts upon my son."

There were so many names that he soon became hoarse repeating the time-honored words. He had just reached the end of the second page when he was told that guests had already begun to arrive and were waiting impatiently in the Great Hall, grumbling that nobody was there to receive them.

The King tossed the list away, clutched his heart, and rushed into the Great Hall to greet his guests. He bowed and scraped and pleaded for their goodwill. He was so apologetic that most of the company pitied him, and promised that they would do his son no harm.

But one Enchantress frowned at his excuses. All she could think of was that no one had been there to welcome her or help her alight from the great ostrich on which she'd traveled from her distant home. She began muttering to herself in a way that alarmed not only the King but all who overheard her malicious remarks.

"Talk is cheap!" she said to the King. "You and your apologies! Talk, talk, talk! Your son will never be anything to boast of! He will be nothing but a manikin—"

She would have wished a dozen other afflictions on the innocent baby Prince if it hadn't been for the good Fairy Genesta, who held the kingdom of the foolish King and Queen under her special protection. Genesta calmed the angry Enchantress. She praised the great ostrich that had brought the Enchantress so swiftly across the seas and persuaded her to say no more. Then, turning to the King, the Fairy Genesta hinted that now was the time to distribute the presents. When this was done the entire company, except for Genesta, left the palace. Most of them flew, but others simply vanished, disappearing into thin air.

Genesta went directly to the Queen and said: "A nice mess you've made of this christening! Why didn't you consult me? Foolish people like you always think they can do without any help or advice. Even worse, forgetting all my goodness to you these many years, you even forgot to invite me to the christening of the little Prince."

"Ah, dear Genesta," cried the King, throwing himself at her feet. "We invited you but the list was so long I never got to the page with your name. Please, look at it yourself! Do you see this mark on the bottom of the second page? That was when I gave up the whole hopeless business!"

"There, there!" said the Fairy. "I'm not offended. I don't allow myself to be put out by trifles with people I'm really fond of. But now we must talk about your son. I've managed to save him from a great many dangers, but you've made an enemy who will never forget the insult to her precious pride. The little Prince will never be safe in this palace. You must let me take him away. And listen carefully to these words of mine. You will not see your son again until he is all covered with fur!"

At these mysterious words the King and Queen burst into tears. The Fairy's prediction shriveled their foolish yet loving hearts. They couldn't imagine how or why their son should come to be covered with fur like some wild animal. Their kingdom had never known snow or ice. Month in and month out, the weather was always hot. The Fairy Genesta told them to dry their tears and to trust in her powers.

"If I left him to you to bring up," said she, "you would be certain to make him as foolish as yourselves. Why, I won't

even let him know he is your son! As for you, Your Majesties, it is high time that you learn how to govern properly!"

So saying, she opened the window, and picking up the cradle in which the little Prince was sleeping, she glided away in the air as if she were skating on ice.

When the King and Queen had recovered a little from the shock of that terrible day, they consulted everyone in the palace as to what the Fairy had meant by saying: *You will not see your son again until he is all covered with fur.*

Nobody, not even the wisest of their ministers, could think of a satisfactory answer. All agreed, however, that it was a frightening statement. More miserable than ever, the King and the Queen absented themselves from the Court. Day after day they wandered through their magnificent chambers like two ghosts searching for a treasure lost forever.

Meanwhile, the Fairy Genesta had carried off the royal baby to her own castle. She placed him under the care of a peasant woman who lived in a nearby village and whom she had bewitched; the woman thought that this new baby was one of her own children. The wise Fairy had decided that the little son of the foolish King and Queen could only benefit if he was brought up as a young peasant boy.

He grew healthy and strong. He spoke what was in his heart, and his heart was good. When he reached manhood Genesta took him to her castle where she herself became his teacher. Under her guidance his mind was exercised as his body had been during his years as a peasant boy. His education didn't stop there. Genesta had resolved that he must soon go out into the world to be tested by hardship and disappointment. Experience alone could give him what no book could give: knowledge of his fellow men. In Genesta's opinion, this was especially necessary for the Prince because in stature he was unusually small.

The ill-tempered Enchantress had dwarfed his natural growth. He was in truth a manikin. In spite of this handicap, he was so well formed, so handsome and soft-spoken, that after a few minutes his size didn't matter to most people. His gentle manners won the hearts of all who responded to goodness. As for Manikin, as he was called by everybody, he didn't delude himself. Was his name ridiculous? So it was! Someday, he consoled himself, if he were given the opportunity, he would make it illustrious.

The ever-watchful Genesta, pleased by her pupil's character, by his honesty and courage, readied him for the world outside her castle by conjuring up wonderful dreams when he slept. Dreams of great adventures on the sea and land in which he always figured as the hero. Sometimes he dreamed that through brave deeds he had earned a kingdom, or had rescued a lovely Princess from some terrible danger. The dreams made him restless; he longed to make them come true. He imagined himself riding out of the castle with its high walls to some distant and dangerous country. There, at the ends of the earth, his humble birth would be no bar to fame and fortune.

At last the Fairy Genesta kissed Manikin good-bye. The little adventurer, his heart overflowing with dreams, rode out into the surrounding forest. He wore the simple clothes of a hunter, and was armed with a bow and arrows and a light spear. Above him the sun shone through the thick leaves, and where the forest ended a trail led to the great city where the foolish King and Queen ruled over their kingdom.

He entered the main gate as he had done in years past—a peasant boy carrying vegetables to sell to the city folk. He saw that everybody, or so it seemed—men, women, and children—were hurrying toward the marketplace. His curiosity was aroused. On reaching the marketplace he skillfully guided his horse through the press of people. They were looking at a group of men dressed in strange foreign clothes who stood on a high wooden platform. As Manikin approached, one of their number, an old man richly dressed like an ambassador, began to address the crowd:

"Let the whole world know that the man who can climb to the summit of the Ice Mountain shall receive as his reward, not only the incomparable Princess Sabella, fariest of the fair, but also all the realms of which she is Queen!"

After proclaiming these words, the old man held up a sheet of paper that reached almost to his knees and said:

"Here is the list of all those Princes who, dazzled by the beauty of the Princess Sabella, have perished in the attempt to win her hand

and her heart. And here on this second list are the names of all those who have elected themselves as contenders."

Manikin was seized with a violent desire to add his own name but when he thought of how poor he was, a peasant born, he hesitated.

The old man motioned to his attendants, who stepped forward with a veiled painting. He uncovered it, and the crowd gasped with admiration. It was a portrait of the Princess Sabella. She was indeed as the old man had said, the "fairest of the fair." One glance was enough for Manikin. He rushed forward to write his name on the list. The richly dressed foreigner stared at the little man in his simple hunting clothes, not knowing whether to accept or to reject him as a contender.

"Give me the list that I may sign it!" Manikin demanded. Reluctantly they obeyed. He was so overcome by his emotions—fascinated by the beautiful portrait and infuriated with the hesitant foreigners—that he couldn't think of any other name except the one by which he'd always been known. Pen in hand, he found a space below the grand names and grand titles and wrote: *Manikin.*

"Manikin!" the old man's attendants cried out, shaking with laughter. "Manikin!"

"Miserable wretches!" Manikin shouted. "If not for this beautiful lady in the painting, I'd cut off your heads!"

No sooner had he uttered this terrible threat when he remembered that, after all, it was a funny name, and that he hadn't yet had time to make it famous. So he smiled and politely asked for directions to the country of the Princess Sabella.

"Four hundred leagues north of Mount Caucasus," he was told. "There you will receive your orders and instructions for the conquest of the Ice Mountain."

To say the least, these directions to a country located near present-day Japan weren't very clear. But Manikin resolved to set out at once, without saying good-bye to his protectress, the Fairy Genesta. He was too fearful that she might try to stop him.

As he galloped away from the marketplace many a citizen joked at Manikin's ridiculous ambitions. The hand of the Princess Sabella no less! What would the Princess say when she cast her beautiful eyes down at a man so tiny she could if she wished lift him up into her arms like a baby! They laughed at his dream of conquering the Ice Mountain where so many bigger and stronger adventurers had perished.

"The Ice Mountain!" they jeered. "Let Manikin first conquer a molehill!"

For the first time in his life Manikin was talked about by everybody. The gossip even reached the ears of the foolish King and Queen, who laughed as loudly as their subjects had done, without knowing, of course, that the butt of the laughter was their only son.

On leaving the city Manikin rode eastward, avoiding towns where he might encounter still other taunts. He hadn't yet won the serenity of a man who could enjoy a joke against himself. At night he slept in the woods and in the morning searched for berries and nuts to eat. It was no fare for an active man, and Manikin was always hungry.

The Fairy Genesta, however, who like all Fairies could be in several places at the same time, was keeping a watchful eye on her half-starved ward. Wild berries were well and good but not sufficient fare for a man constantly on horseback. So while he slept she took to feeding him with all sorts of nourishing foods. On awaking he often wondered why he never felt hungry but strong and hearty as if he had dined on roast venison and good bread.

When he had lived in Genesta's castle, she had conjured up dreams of adventure. In the country where he now found himself, they soon took on real shape and form. He fought with bandits and outlaws; he was attacked by wild beasts and even wilder monsters. His fighting ability was tested in these combats and struggles, and although he was the victor he learned that there was often a price for victory. He lost his faithful horse in a fight with a monster with a tigerlike head. Sadly, Manikin placed a flower between the eyes of his horse and continued his journey on foot.

At last he reached a seaport. One of the ships was about to sail in the direction in which he wanted to go. He spoke to the captain and paid for his passage with his remaining coins. The first few days at sea were calm, but then a storm ripped the sails and snapped the masts. The ship foundered in the crashing waves and began to sink. The lifeboats capsized, and the crew and passengers had to swim for their lives. Manikin would have drowned if the waves hadn't subsided. In the distance he could see a dim shore. When he crawled up on the beach, he collapsed and slept like the dead. But the dead are dreamless—and Manikin dreamed of Ice Mountains as many as the waves and, raising her head like a mermaid, the Princess Sabella smiled at him with teeth white as snow. . . .

Manikin awoke at dawn. He soon discovered that he was marooned on a desert island. He was all alone. The days passed. He lived by fishing and hunting, always hoping that the good Fairy Genesta would rescue him. For brave as he was, there are situations in which even the bravest among us are helpless. One day, as he was looking out to sea, he saw an oddly shaped boat drifting toward the shore. He watched it enter a little creek where it stopped, stuck fast in sand and mud.

Shouting with joy, he rushed down the hill toward the boat. When he got close he was astonished to see that the masts looked like trees and the spars like branches. The boat itself was thickly covered with leaves and seemed like a small floating woods. He called, but no one answered him. There wasn't a sound on board; it was as if the crew had deserted their strange vessel. Manikin pushed the branches aside and leaped onto the deck. What he saw now would have shaken a giant, let alone a manikin. The crew hadn't deserted. Mute and silent, they lay sprawled across the deck like the living dead. Even more shocking, they were changing before Manikin's eyes into trees! Roots grew out of their bodies, fastening them to the deck, to the masts, or to whatever else they had happened to be touching when the enchantment fell upon them. Manikin's eyes dimmed with tears of pity at their awful fate. Then, rousing himself, he hurried to set them free. With the sharp point of one of his arrows he gently cut through the woody growth that held their hands and feet.

One by one he carried them ashore where he rubbed their stiffened wooden limbs. Later that morning he bathed them with a concoction made from healing herbs he found on the island. In a few days the enchanted crew had recovered the use of both their bodies and their minds.

You may be sure that the ever-watchful Fairy Genesta had something to do with this marvelous cure! Who but she inspired Manikin to rub the boat itself with the same magical herbs, arresting its transformation into a woods! The thickening trunks and sprouting branches melted away. Once again neat and trim, the boat floated free and clean. The grateful sailors offered to land their rescuer wherever he pleased, but before the sails were unfurled, he questioned them for hours. They couldn't explain what had happened to their vessel or to themselves. All they knew was that a sudden gust of wind had reached them from the land as they were passing a densely wooded coast. It had enveloped them in a strange, opaque cloud. After that, everything on the boat that wasn't metal began to change. They themselves had grown numb and heavy and began to lose consciousness.

Their story fascinated Manikin. Thinking it over, he collected some of the dust from the bottom of the boat. Its magical properties, he thought, might be a handy thing to have someday.

Joyfully they left the island where Manikin had been marooned. After a long and uneventful voyage, they sighted land. The anchor was dropped, and two small boats were lowered. They rowed ashore to take on a fresh stock of water and provisions and to find out, if they could, where they were. As they neared the shore they could see no houses and no human beings, and yet they knew they had been observed by living things. For they glimpsed a number of small dark shapes, dimly visible within little dust clouds rolling across the ground. The mysterious creatures seemed to be rushing toward the exact spot where the two small boats were preparing to go ashore. As the oarsmen raced across the water the small dark shapes on the shore became distinct and unmistakable.

Manikin and the sailors stared with bulging eyes at an army of large, beautiful spaniels! Some were sentries, others grouped into companies and regiments. Manikin leaped ashore and greeted the spaniels in a friendly way. They crowded around him with a great wagging of tails and a giving of paws, nuzzling against his legs and pointing with their noses as if to say: *Follow us!*

Manikin guessed that they wanted only him to go with them. He was more than willing. He arranged with the sailors to wait fifteen days; if he failed to return by then, they were to hoist sail and continue on their voyage without him. The sailors warned Manikin to be careful. He replied that he trusted his new companions.

The spaniels led him inland, away from the shore and the sea. They passed fields, which to Manikin's amazement were cultivated. He couldn't believe his eyes when he saw his first plowman, or rather, plowdog. The plows were drawn by horses but guided by spaniels! After awhile he became accustomed to the sights of this strange world; the horse-drawn carts and carriages; the prosperous villages. When they paused to rest, a fine meal was prepared. While Manikin ate, a chariot was readied with two splendid horses in the shafts and a coal-black spaniel for a driver.

The journey was continued in comfort. When they passed a carriage on the road, the drivers raised their paws in friendly salute. News of their coming had evidently been received in the capital of this kingdom of spaniels. For when they drove into the city, the inhabitants were standing at their doors or looking out from their windows. Perched on walls and gates, the little spaniels, more excited than their parents, wagged their tails so fast they seemed like whips. Manikin, delighted with the hearty welcome, waved his hand in greeting.

His driver turned down a wide paved avenue shaded by rows of fine trees. At the end of it a magnificent palace towered into the blue sky. They entered a courtyard, and Manikin returned the salutes of the spaniel-soldiers stationed along the walls. A few minutes later he was ushered into the presence of the King, a large and very beautiful spaniel. His Majesty was lying on a rich Persian carpet surrounded by several spaniels who, like dutiful pages, were engaged in chasing away flies hovering over their monarch.

The King, who had been gazing at this stranger from a distant land with a sad look in his eyes, sprang up now to welcome his visitor. Then, raising his paw, he motioned to his courtiers. One by one they paid their respects to the unexpected visitor.

Manikin had been wondering how he would carry on a conversation, but once he and the King were alone, a wise-looking spaniel—the Secretary of State—trotted into the royal chamber. From the jeweled pouch around his neck he took out a sheaf of paper, an inkwell, and a quill pen. As His Majesty dictated in dog language, the Secretary wrote down his words, none of which were comprehensible to Manikin. The speech was then given to Manikin to read. He was astonished to see that it was written in human language. His Majesty had dictated that he was sorry they could talk only in writing since the language of dogs was difficult to understand. However, he wanted his visitor to know that he was welcome and would be accorded all honors and courtesies.

Manikin thanked the King and wrote a polite reply; he asked His Majesty to satisfy his curiosity about all the strange

things he'd seen and heard since his arrival. This request appeared to sadden the King of Spaniels. His head dropped, and he seemed to be lost in thought. Then, with a shake, he roused himself and dictated a lengthy explanation. His name was King Bayard, and not so long ago he'd been as human as his visitor. His misfortunes were caused by a Fairy whose kingdom was next to his own. She had fallen in love with him, but how could he marry her when his heart belonged to the Queen of the Spice Islands? The Fairy, furious at his confession, had reduced him to the state in which his visitor found him. The jealous Fairy had left him unchanged in mind but deprived of human speech.

Not content with punishing him alone, she had condemned all his subjects to a similar fate, saying: *Bark and run upon four feet, until the time comes when virtue shall be rewarded with love and fortune.*

This, as the unhappy King Bayard dictated to his Secretary, was very much the same thing as if she'd said: "Remain a spaniel forever and ever."

Manikin sympathized with the unfortunate King. He had seen enough of the world to realize that wickedness rather than virtue usually gained what men prized. He felt very sorry for the King, advised him to be patient, and promised to help him with all his might if the chance arose. In no time at all they had become close friends. The King proudly showed Manikin a portrait of the lovely Queen of the Spice

Islands. And Manikin in turn told his own history. His life, he said, was worthless to him if he failed in his great undertaking. The love of the beautiful Sabella was all that mattered. But first he must travel to the kingdom where she lived, north of Mount Caucasus.

"I can be of some help," said the King. "I will send for maps and advise the Captain of your boat on the navigation."

Together they traveled to the anchored craft. The Captain and crew cheered when they saw Manikin. They thanked the King for the supplies his spaniels carried on board. As another proof of abiding friendship, Bayard insisted that Manikin take with him one of his own pages, an unusually clever spaniel whose name was Mousta. Mousta would attend to Manikin's wants and serve him faithfully. At last the moment to say good-bye could no longer be postponed. The King and Manikin embraced each other and parted.

The sails were unfurled, and the little boat glided out into the unknown. Soon they were far out from land and could no longer hear the great howl of regret from the army of assembled spaniels—as a compliment to his new friend and ally, King Bayard had commanded his subjects to bay with all their might.

Day followed day. The sun rose and sank in the waters; the winds were favorable; and guided by King Bayard's instructions, they finally sighted the harbor that was their destination. Since Manikin had no money left in his purse,

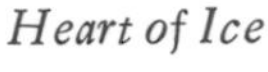

he decided to avoid the port. With Mousta, he was rowed to the shore. There he said a sad good-bye to the crew he had rescued from a terrible fate. After many farewells, Manikin called to Mousta. The spaniel sniffed at the breeze and pointed out a promising direction.

Mousta trotted ahead of Manikin. Tall trees shaded them from the sun, and when they tired they rested in a green meadow in the middle of the forest. It was so pleasant here after their long, tiring voyage that they lingered on, stretching out in the green, cool shade of the leaves. A wind blew among the ferns, and the sharp-eyed Mousta spied a little monkey in the branches overhead. They watched it jump from limb to limb. Then, head over heels, it tumbled through the foliage like an acrobat until it stood on the ground. It was so pretty that Manikin sprang up and tried to catch it.

The monkey, just keeping out of arm's reach, called to Manikin over its soft furry shoulder: "Will you promise to follow me wherever I lead?"

Manikin was astonished that this tiny creature had the gift of human speech. He was even more astonished when the monkey leaped to his shoulder and whispered in his ear:

"We monkeys have no money either, poor Manikin. We are so poor we don't know what to do next."

"And I have nothing to give you," he answered regretfully. "No sugar or biscuits or anything that you might like."

"Since you are so considerate about me, and so patient about your own undertaking," said the little monkey, "I will show you the way to the Golden Rock. But you must leave Mousta here until you return."

Manikin nodded his agreement. The little monkey hopped from his shoulder to the nearest tree, calling: "Follow me!"

Nimble as Manikin was, he didn't find this easy. His little guide waited and showed him the easiest paths through the undergrowth. Gradually the trees thinned out and directly before them was a clear grassy space in the middle of which stood a single rock, about ten feet high.

"That stone looks hard," said the little monkey. "Give it a blow with your spear, Manikin, and we'll see what will happen!"

Manikin raised his spear and struck at the rock. Several pieces split off, and the astonished spearman saw that the rock was sheathed with a layer of stone, concealing a solid mass of pure gold.

The little monkey laughed: "I make you a present of what you have broken off. Take as much of it as you think right."

Manikin murmured his heartfelt thanks and picked up one of the smallest pieces.

As he did so the little monkey was suddenly transformed into a tall, gracious Fairy, who said to him: "If you are always as kind and easily contented as you are now, you may hope to accomplish the most difficult tasks. Go on your way, Manikin! You will never lack for money. That little lump of gold which you modestly chose will never grow less. But before we part, I want you to see the dangers you have escaped."

The Fairy led him back by another path into a dense woods. Between the trees a crowd of men and women ran about like maniacs, their faces pale and haggard, their eyes fixed on the ground, pushing and trampling each other in their frenzy as they searched for the Golden Rock.

"You see how they suffer!" said the Fairy. "Greed drives them on, but it is all to no avail! They will end up dying of despair as hundreds have before them."

She shook her head as if she could never understand the depths of human greed. Then she brought Manikin back to the place where he'd left Mousta. The faithful spaniel greeted him with joy. When they looked around, the Fairy had disappeared.

Man and dog instantly set off with sure steps. It was as if the Fairy of the Golden Rock were flitting before them to point out the way. They walked through the forest and climbed a high hill. Below, in the distance, they saw the roofs of a large town. Here they stayed for several days. The little piece of gold, as the Fairy had promised, never grew less. Manikin purchased horses and hired attendants, and when he asked for directions to the distant kingdom of the Princess Sabella, the townfolk listened respectfully to the rich newcomer.

After a long and tiresome journey, Manikin and his party reached Mount Caucasus. Here there was no need to ask any questions. The people spoke of nothing else but the Princess. She lived, they said, in the great city of Trelintin, four hundred leagues to the north. She was the most beautiful woman who had ever lived. Her eyes were bluer than the bluest sky, her hair surpassed the golden rays of the sun. Her wealth was so vast that it would take a thousand men a thousand years to count her gold and silver and jewels. There were a hundred stories about the innumerable great Princes and powerful Kings from all parts of the world who sought her hand in marriage.

One King marched with an army at his back. Another was almost as rich as the Princess herself. A third had so many grand titles he could scarcely remember them all.

Manikin listened to these tales about his rivals and remembered that he had no titles of any kind, only his ridiculous name. His army consisted of his hired attendants. He had no knights but his loyal spaniel, Mousta, and his own knightly resolve to win the heart of the beautiful Sabella.

"Tomorrow we leave," he said to Mousta.

Two whole months would pass before they came to Trelintin, the capital of the kingdom, of which Sabella was the shining star. Manikin's pleasure at walking the streets and avenues where Sabella, perhaps mounted on a jeweled horse, had ridden by gave way to anxiety when he listened to the stories of the inhabitants.

The Ice Mountain!

Night and day he heard that heart-chilling phrase! The Ice

Mountain that no man could climb and from which no suitor of Sabella's had ever returned! The Ice Mountain more dangerous than a dragon! The Ice Mountain, devourer of men!

SABELLA'S FATHER, King Farda-Kinbras, and her mother, the beautiful Queen Birbantine, had once been the happiest couple on earth. They ruled over a great and rich kingdom, and in their royal conceit they imagined their joy would continue forever. One day, while blissfully sleigh-riding in a newly fallen snow, they defied fate and spoiled their happiness.

"We shall see about that!" grumbled an old hag who sat by the wayside blowing on her fingers to keep them warm. The King was angered and wanted to punish the hag.

The Queen stopped him: "Sire, let us not make bad worse! I hope I'm mistaken, but I think this is a Fairy!"

"You are not mistaken, Birbantine!" said the old woman as she stood up. And as they gazed at her she grew gigantic, towering over the frightened King and Queen in their sleigh. Her staff turned into a fiery dragon with outstretched wings, her ragged cloak into a golden mantle, her wooden shoes into two bundles of rockets. "You are not mistaken!" the Fairy repeated with a malicious smile. "Soon you will see what comes of your arrogance in defying fate. And you will never forget the Fairy Gorgonzola! Never!"

The King and Queen begged to be forgiven. The Fairy ignored their pleas. Mounting the dragon, she flew off, the rockets bursting behind her and leaving long trails of fiery sparks. The King and Queen wept. The newly fallen snow in which they had rejoiced seemed suddenly sinister like some immense shroud.

Not too long afterward, Queen Birbantine gave birth to a beautiful baby daughter. As was the custom, all the Fairies of the North, including the Fairy Gorgonzola, were invited to the christening. Unseen by anyone, Gorgonzola tiptoed into the palace and watched the company shower the little Princess with their gifts. When the guests were seated at the banquet table, the evil Fairy, disguised as a black cat, crept into the room of the little Princess. She hid under the cradle and waited for the nurses to turn their backs. When they did, she sprang out and in an instant stole the heart of the sleeping child.

She rushed into the courtyard while behind her the dogs barked and a kitchen scullion shouted. No one in the palace, high or low, suspected that anything had happened to spoil the christening; not even the Fairies. Swift as a beam of moonlight, Gorgonzola flew to the North Pole where no living being, whether human, beast, or bird, could endure the terrible cold. No eyes saw her fly to the summit of the Ice Mountain. There she concealed the stolen heart, absolutely certain that it would remain hidden as long as the Princess Sabella lived.

Far to the south, in Trelintin, Sabella blossomed like an

ever-blooming flower. The beautiful child grew into a beautiful woman. She seemed perfect. The King and Queen forgot the old hag who before their eyes had changed into a gigantic Fairy mounted on a fiery dragon. Their daughter was not only beautiful in face and body but also in mind. Her quickness astonished the wisest men in the kingdom. Without the slightest trouble she mastered the contents of the books brought to her by the palace scholars. Yet, as she ripened into womanhood—intelligent, witty, charming—something seemed to be lacking. She had an exquisite voice, but whether her songs were sad or gay, she sang as if she really had no idea of what the words meant.

"She certainly sings perfectly," the courtiers agreed. "But there is no tenderness, no heart in her voice."

Poor Sabella! How could there be when her heart was locked away on the Ice Mountain!

It wasn't only her voice that seemed cold. In spite of the admiration of the entire Court, and the blind fondness of her father and mother, it became more and more evident as time went by that some fatal flaw had marred the beautiful and accomplished Princess. For those poor souls who love no one cannot long be loved.

The unhappy King and Queen finally were forced to face the bitter truth. The King hesitated for months, but at last he invited the Fairies of the North to a general assembly, hoping they might discover the reasons for his daughter's indifference to all who loved her. He praised Sabella's beauty and brilliance; then, wiping his tears, he declared that not only he, but all his counselors, were completely mystified.

"It is certain, dear Fairies," said he, "that something is wrong. *What* it is, I don't know how to tell you, but in some way your efforts on her behalf have failed. I must say that your work was imperfect."

The Fairies assured the King that as far as they knew, Sabella had been given every virtue and talent. For all were grateful to the King, the most generous of monarchs. After this they went to see Sabella.

No sooner had they entered her chamber than they all exclaimed with one voice: "Oh, horror! She has no heart!"

On hearing this frightful outcry, the Queen fainted, and the King, groaning with despair, implored the Fairies to find some cure for such an unheard-of misfortune. The oldest Fairy consulted her *Book of Magic* which she always carried attached to her girdle by a thick silver chain. She thumbed through its pages and almost immediately found out that the wicked Gorgonzola had stolen Sabella's heart and hidden it away on the Ice Mountain.

"What shall we do?" cried the King and Queen in one breath.

"You love her," the oldest Fairy said with pity. "You must suffer dreadfully, and yet what do you love? Your Sabella is nothing but a beautiful image, and this must go on for a long time. But I think from what I've read in my *Book of Magic* that in the end, your beloved daughter will once more regain

her heart. You must send your ambassadors out into the world to tell her story. Her beauty alone is sufficient to attract all the Princes and Kings who dream of beauty. They will risk their lives to gain her hand, and one of them will succeed in climbing the Ice Mountain."

The King and Queen immediately ordered their ambassadors to travel to the capitals of every kingdom to announce that the man who recovered the stolen heart of Sabella would be rewarded with her hand. . . .

WHEN MANIKIN ARRIVED in Trelintin some five hundred Princes with their squires and pages had already perished in the snow and ice. Just the same, countless others dreaming of success rode into the city, cheered by the crowds. Manikin looked on gloomily. Many of his rivals equaled or surpassed the splendor of even the mighty King Farda-Kinbras. They entered the city mounted on magnificent horses, followed by troops of retainers. Manikin was forced to smile. He had dismissed his hired retainers. His faithful Mousta was retainer, knight, squire, and page—all in one.

"Yes, Mousta," he said with a wry smile, "we must take heart! Tomorrow I'll present myself at the Court."

The next day he paid his respects to the King and Queen and asked permission, as was the custom, to go and kiss the hand of the Princess.

King Farda-Kinbras hesitated: "And what are your titles?" he inquired politely.

"I have no titles, Your Majesty! outside of my own valor and courage, and no name but Manikin!"

The King could hardly repress a smile. The haughty and high-born Princes who had already presented themselves shouted with laughter.

Turning toward the King, Manikin said with quiet dignity, "Your Majesty, I'm glad that it is in my power to amuse you. But I'm not a plaything for these gentlemen! I must beg them to treat me with respect, as I treat all with respect, noble or commoner."

There was another mocking shout. Manikin walked over to the Prince who had laughed the loudest and challenged him to a single combat. This Prince, who was called Fadasse, accepted scornfully. He felt sure he would be victorious against so small and insignificant a foe. The meeting was arranged for the next day. Manikin bowed himself out of the royal presence and was conducted to the audience hall of the Princess Sabella.

He looked at her speechlessly. She was more beautiful than the portrait he'd seen so long ago.

"Lovely Princess," he said in a shaky voice, "the beauty of your portrait has brought me here from the other end of the earth to offer my services. My devotion to you has no limits, but my absurd name has already involved me in a quarrel with

one of your suitors, the Prince Fadasse. Tomorrow I will fight this ugly and overgrown Prince! I beg you to honor the combat with your presence, Princess. By so doing, you will show the world that there is nothing in a name, and that a royal Princess with as many titles as there are pearls around your neck is not too proud to accept Manikin as your knight."

The Princess was amused by the proposal. For, although she had no heart, she was not without humor. She glanced at the challenger. Although he was mouselike in size, she thought that he spoke with the voice of a noble cat.

"I will be pleased," she said, "to accept you as my knight, Manikin."

Delighted by her response, Manikin thanked the Princess and said: "I have no right to ask, but ask I must. I would be the happiest man on earth if you would be so kind as not to show any favor to the overgrown Fadasse."

"I favor none of these foolish courtiers, Manikin. I'm tired of their sentiment and their folly! I'm tired of hearing all their declarations of undying love! Love! What a dull thing that must be! I do very well as I am. Yet, from one year's end to another, they talk of nothing but saving me from some imaginary spell that has blinded me to love and romance and who knows what other dull things besides? Who can remember all their nonsense?"

She had spoken not from the heart—for she had no heart—but from her mind. Manikin, although shocked by her speech, immediately realized it would be useless to add himself to the list of his rivals who spoke of nothing but love. To Sabella, the language of love was as mysterious and incomprehensible as the secret language of the Fairies was to any mortal. He had a feeling that it would be better to amuse her if he wished to gain her favor.

"What isn't nonsense?" he smiled.

The next day, at the hour appointed for the combat, the King and Queen and Princess took their places in the stands. The courtiers seated themselves on silk cushions. The people who had neither titles nor seats stood on their feet, crowded together so tightly they formed a wall of faces.

Prince Fadasse rode into the lists, followed by twenty-four squires and a hundred men-at-arms, each one leading a spirited horse. Manikin, whose only weapon was a spear, with Mousta at his heels, entered from the opposite end. The contrast between the two rivals was so great that the entire assembly burst into laughter.

The trumpets sounded, and the two rivals rushed upon each other. Eluding the blow aimed at his head, Manikin thrust Prince Fadasse down from his horse and pinned him to the sand with his spear. It had all happened so fast that no one could believe what they saw with their own eyes. The laughter stopped, and a murmur of admiration rose from the stands. The little victor crossed over to where the Princess was seated. He bowed and said that he lacked the heart to kill anyone who called himself a suitor for her hand.

His speech pleased the spectators. And when Manikin told

the angry and humiliated Fadasse to rise and thank the Princess Sabella, to whom he owed his life, the applause was deafening. From all sides there was praise for the victor whose gallantry in combat was matched by his gallantry with words.

That same day the King sent for Manikin and offered his congratulations. Then he invited Manikin to live in the palace until his turn came to leave Trelintin for the Ice Mountain.

Overjoyed at the thought of being so near the lovely Sabella, Manikin said modestly, "I don't deserve this great honor, Your Majesty, but my heart bids me to accept."

The next few weeks were the happiest in his life. He strolled in the gardens with the Princess, and they met at meals. When the beautiful Sabella laughed at her suitors who spoke of nothing but love, Manikin pretended that he, too, thought love folly. He pointed out the imperfections of his rivals. And since every human being is far from perfect, he found in each of them some trait or character he could joke about.

Prince Fadasse, he said, spent hours in his dressing room. Another high-born Prince was always served wild game when he dined, believing that venison made him swift of foot and that bear meat gave him strength.

Sabella was amused by Manikin's stories. He succeeded so well in entertaining the Princess that soon she declared that of all the people at the Court, he was the one to whom she preferred to talk.

"Manikin," she said one day, "I have heard that your

spaniel, Mousta, is the cleverest dog in the kingdom, which doesn't surprise me. Like master, like dog," she smiled. "I would like to see this paragon."

Manikin consented gladly. The Princess wasn't disappointed. Mousta's fine manners and marvelous intelligence captivated Sabella, and before long she wanted the dog for her own pet. Manikin was only too pleased to grant her wish, not merely out of politeness, but because he foresaw the advantage of having a faithful friend always near the Princess.

His friendship with Sabella impressed the entire Court. He had become an important figure, and although one or two courtiers still scorned Manikin, they were too fearful of his prowess in battle to voice what was in their minds. If his stature was short and his name absurd, nevertheless he had defeated the Prince Fadasse so quickly that people were still open-mouthed with wonder.

Soon after, the ambassador of the powerful King Brandatimor arrived at the frontier and sent a letter to the palace requesting an immediate reply and permission to enter the capital:

"I, Brandatimor, greet the worthy King Farda-Kinbras, the father of the beautiful Sabella. If I had seen her portrait before it was seen by so many adventurers and petty Princes, I would have whipped them away from your great city like a pack of dogs, and by so doing saved their skins from getting frozen in their foolish attempts to climb the Ice Mountain. Worthy Farda-Kinbras, I intend to marry your daughter.

My ambassador has orders, therefore, to make arrangements for the Princess to come and be married to me without delay. I attach no importance whatsoever to the nonsense about this Ice Mountain which you have caused to be published throughout the world.

"If the Princess Sabella really has no heart, be assured that it doesn't bother me in the least. For if anybody can help her to discover one, it is I Brandatimor. I have written clearly what I feel in my own heart, so, my worthy father-in-law, farewell."

Brandatimor's imperious letter angered the King and Queen. The Princess was furious at the contempt it revealed for her father and mother and for herself. All three agreed that its contents must be kept secret until they could decide on a reply. But Mousta, who had been present during the discussion, informed Manikin of all that had been said. Immediately Manikin asked for an audience with Sabella. When they met, he skillfully led the conversation up to the subject that agitated her.

Wringing her lovely hands, Sabella denounced Brandatimor and his insolent letter. "You must advise me, Manikin, about the best course of action," she said in a distressed voice.

"We must gain a little time," he replied. "Why don't you promise an answer after you've spoken to Brandatimor's ambassador? In the meanwhile your father could grant him permission to enter the city."

The ambassador had expected Sabella's immediate consent

to a marriage with his master. From his quarters on the frontier he dispatched a threatening letter of his own. He wrote that as soon as his retainers and men-at-arms arrived, he intended to march into the capital and show the rabble of petty Princes who dared ask for the hand of the Princess Sabella the power and magnificence of King Brandatimor. Let them beware!

Manikin, after reading the ambassador's brutal letter, felt his heart grow cold as if an icy fragment from the Ice Mountain had lodged in his chest. In his despair he was tempted to call on the Fairy Genesta. Often he'd thought of her and always with gratitude. But from the moment when he'd left her castle, he had resolved not to seek her aid but to rely on himself alone.

That night when he fell asleep, worn out from thinking about Brandatimor and the iron-fisted ambassador who aped his master, he dreamed that Genesta stood beside his bed speaking in a low voice:

"Manikin, you have done very well so far. Continue to please me and you shall always find good friends when you need them most. You can assure Sabella that she needn't fear the triumphant entry of Brandatimor's conceited ambassador. All will turn out well for her in the end."

Manikin tried to throw himself at Genesta's feet, only he woke up. It was all a dream, he thought. Just the same, he felt calm and confident. When he spoke with Sabella he was his old courageous self again. He said that men far more powerful than Brandatimor had been humbled. He hinted that he, Manikin, would be the instrument of deliverance. He even ventured to ask the anxious Princess if she wouldn't be grateful once she was rid of the vainglorious Brandatimor. Sabella replied that her gratitude would be unlimited. At these words Manikin's heart began to beat so rapidly he felt dizzy. When he could speak, he wanted to know how she would reward the person, perhaps himself, lucky enough to outwit or outfight Brandatimor.

"What would you wish for him, Princess?" said he, trembling. "What would your best wish be?"

"I would wish him to be as indifferent to this folly called *love* as I am myself."

Sabella's answer almost brought tears to Manikin's eyes, but with an effort he managed to conceal his pain.

That very day, word arrived in the palace that Brandatimor's ambassador was marching on the capital. He would arrive in the morning, and he warned that there must be no more delays. The great King he served was impatient; the marriage must take place immediately so that Brandatimor could turn his attention to the many urgent affairs of state he had neglected.

From early dawn the people of Trelintin were awake. By the thousands they lined the main avenue, waiting to see the great army of Brandatimor. No one in the crowd suspected that the Fairy Genesta had cast a spell on every man, woman, and child. She had bewitched the eyes of everyone. When the ambassador's procession came into sight—and it was truly a splendid procession!—the enchanted spectators *saw* a parade of beggars. The gorgeous uniforms of the generals seemed like miserable rags; the prancing horses appeared as wretched skeletons hardly able to drag one foot after another. Although their saddles and trappings sparkled with jewels and gold, they *looked* like old sheepskins that wouldn't have been good enough for a plow horse. The men-at-arms in their plumed steel helmets *looked* like kitchen scullions; the elegant pages, like chimney sweeps. The trumpets sounded like whistles made out of onion stalks or combs wrapped in paper. The train of fifty carriages pulled by horses any King would have been proud to own *looked* like farmers' carts drawn by bedraggled donkeys. In the last creaking cart (so it *appeared* to the astonished multitude) Brandatimor's ambassador sat stiffly, his face fixed in a scornful expression which he considered becoming as the representative of so powerful a monarch.

All who marched—generals, men-at-arms, pages—wore such looks. The parade of beggars, as they now seemed to the onlookers, was greeted with laughter and howls of derision. The crowd hooted and whistled and shouted insults at the ambassador and his army of scarecrows.

"Look at them!" they yelled. "Who do they think they are! Puffed up with pride and vanity like sheep bladders!"

King Farda-Kinbras's messengers, enchanted like all his other subjects, galloped to the palace where the King and Queen were anxiously waiting in the audience hall.

"Your Majesties!" the messengers said breathlessly. "It's an unbelievable sight! Ragamuffins on horseback, if they can be called horses! And yet Brandatimor's knights pretend that their mounts are pure-blooded steeds of Araby. It's a mockery, Your Majesties! Their ambassador fancies that he can force you to swallow this new insult!"

Furious at what he had been told, Farda-Kinbras ordered the palace gates to be shut. He refused to receive Brandatimor's ambassador, who rose in his carriage—for it was a splendid carriage and *not* a farmer's cart—brandishing his sword at the iron gates and crying out that Farda-Kinbras would regret this day. His denunciations enraged the crowds in the square fronting on the palace. They shook their fists and picked up stones and handfuls of mud to pelt the ambassador and his generals.

Dodging the stones, and spattered with mud, the ambassador screamed: "In the name of the mighty King I serve, I declare war against this kingdom of mudslingers! We will return and devastate this land with fire and sword!"

The crowd roared with laughter—to their enchanted eyes the bemedaled ambassador *looked* like an old church beggar—and threw whatever came into their hands.

Behind the locked gates of the palace, King Farda-Kinbras had summoned his ministers to the Council Chamber. No one

could understand why Brandatimor, who after all was a suitor for Sabella's hand, if an arrogant one, should stoop to so base an insult.

"Are we beggars," one minister asked, "that they should come to us masked as beggars?"

The declaration of war, however, presented no riddles. The tyrannous Brandatimor, as they all knew, fully intended to invade the land and destroy it if he could. The King issued orders to his generals to prepare for battle. Every able-bodied man was mustered. Princes who were about to leave for the Ice Mountain postponed their departure and offered their services. Since they all thought highly of themselves, they demanded the best appointments in the army.

Modest as ever, Manikin, one of the first to volunteer, only asked to be an aide-de-camp to the King's Commander in Chief, a famous soldier who had fought in a dozen campaigns.

As soon as he was accepted, Manikin hurried to his chambers to write a letter to King Bayard. First, he reread Bayard's own letter which lay on his desk. It had arrived several weeks ago. Bayard, a true friend, had wanted to know whether Manikin had been lucky or unlucky in his quest; he had promised any assistance in his power if ever called upon.

Manikin picked up a pen and began to write. He described his adventures, praised Mousta, and ended his letter with an account of the deadly quarrel between Brandatimor and Farda-Kinbras. Help was indeed needed! If Bayard could spare several thousand of his veteran spaniels, he, Manikin, would remember this to his dying day!

The peaceful capital had become an armed camp. The news from the frontier was ominous. Brandatimor himself had assumed command of his huge army. Furious at the treatment given to his ambassador, he had sworn he would smash the kingdom of Farda-Kinbras like a bird's egg, reduce Trelintin to rubble and ashes, and carry off the Princess Sabella to his own capital.

The defending army marched to the frontier. When their Commander in Chief saw the great force of the enemy, far outnumbering his own, he ordered his troops to hold their ground and to refrain from attack. With a tremendous shout the battle began. Brandatimor's archers darkened the sky with their arrows. His knights charged, the hooves of their horses louder than thunder. The defenders retreated, but wherever they could, they slashed at the enemy's flanks. Small victories were won, Manikin surrounded and defeated a company of foot soldiers; by nightfall, when the fighting ceased, he'd gained the respect of his fellow officers and the admiration of his soldiers.

The next morning Brandatimor ordered his whole army to attack. The defenders fought desperately, and many an officer was killed, including the brave Commander in Chief. But there seemed to be no end to the invaders. For every one that fell, a dozen others sprang up armed with sword, spear, and lance. Surrounded on all sides, the defenders were beaten back. Here and there the retreat turned into a rout. Half a dozen times Manikin appealed to the panicked troops to hold their ground.

"Winter is coming!" the valiant Manikin cried. "The snows will stop the fighting! We can save Trelintin if we can establish a defensive line! Fight for your King and country! Fight for your wives and children!"

The enemy was checked. Only then did Manikin ride back to Trelintin to report to Farda-Kinbras. The King was heart-broken when he was told of the death of his trusty Commander in Chief. But when his generals praised Manikin's prowess, he felt as if all hadn't been lost. He asked the little Prince to assume command of the army.

The first snows had already covered the capital. Palace and mansion, house and hut, newly roofed with white, gleamed in the sun. The wintry winds blew through the icy streets. All seemed peaceful in Trelintin, but no one knew when the tyrannous Brandatimor would give the command to renew the battle.

Manikin saw Sabella every day, but he didn't neglect his duties as the new Commander in Chief. When his messengers brought word that King Bayard's veteran spaniels had arrived, he instantly sent orders to his four-footed soldiers. They were to post themselves along the frontier without attracting the attention of the enemy patrols.

The chief officer of the spaniels, an old and experienced soldier, journeyed to the capital and advised against a defensive war.

Manikin replied: "Those are my very thoughts, sir. The enemy must be shattered at his first advance, or Trelintin is doomed."

Far from the capital, King Brandatimor inspected his mighty forces. He had no doubts that the final victory would be his, and that he, the mighty Brandatimor, would raise his banners over Trelintin.

"The Princess Sabella will be my bride!" he boasted to his generals, and raising his sword he shouted: "On to Trelintin!"

No sooner had he given the command to charge than Bayard's spaniels, who had mingled with Brandatimor's troops unnoticed, leaped at the throats of the galloping knights. The spaniels dragged the riders from their mounts and turned the riderless beasts to the rear. The frenzied horses galloped into the ranks of the men-at-arms who, wild with terror, tossed their weapons aside and fled.

Manikin and his party rode through the retreating army, searching for Brandatimor. When they encountered him, the furious leader challenged Manikin to single combat.

"I will cut you in two!" Brandatimor roared. "Small as you are, you will be even smaller!"

Brandatimor was far the stronger, but his opponent was quick as a cat. He slipped between Brandatimor's sword thrusts and unhorsed him.

"So the mighty fall!" Manikin cried. He commanded that Brandatimor be taken to the capital.

The fierce monarch didn't live to reach the Court. He couldn't bear the thought of appearing before Sabella as a helpless prisoner of war. Heartbroken, he fell to the ground, killed by his own pride.

Great was the rejoicing in Trelintin. King Farda-Kinbras bestowed new honors on his victorious Commander in Chief. Nobles and commoners all praised Manikin as their savior. His rivals for the hand of Sabella, however, were glum and unhappy. They feared that the mighty little Commander in Chief might prove as successful in conquering the Ice Mountain as he'd been in all his undertakings. One by one they stole out of Trelintin without waiting their turn, traveling northward to the Ice Mountain as swiftly as they could.

When Manikin heard that Prince Fadasse and so many others had treacherously left the city, violating the rules of turn and turnabout, he called on the King and Queen and announced his intentions. They begged him to stay in Trelintin. News had just come to the palace that Prince Fadasse and many others had lost their lives.

"The Ice Mountain!" the King said sadly. "It will never be climbed by mortal man. Poor Sabella's fate is sealed forever. Never will she know the meaning of love."

The unhappy Manikin could only nod in agreement. True, Sabella admired his military deeds. She praised his courage and swore she would never forget the hero who had saved, not only herself, but also the entire kingdom from the brutal Brandatimor. But she showed no signs of returning Manikin's ardent love.

"Your Majesties," Manikin replied, "come what may, I must try to climb the Ice Mountain. What else has brought me to your kingdom?"

That same day he said good-bye to the assembled Court and finally to the Princess Sabella. She gave him her hand to kiss with the same gracious indifference she had shown at their first meeting. Her coldness and lack of heart shocked and outraged the courtiers. They whispered among themselves.

The distressed King turned to Manikin and said: "You have constantly refused all the gifts I have offered you in my gratitude for your heroic services. But now, noble Manikin, I will ask the Princess Sabella to present you with her cloak of marten's fur, and *that* I hope you will not reject!"

Sabella's cloak was a splendid fur mantle. She was very fond of it, not so much because of its warmth, but because its richness set off to perfection the delicate tints of her complexion and the brilliant gold of her hair. The Princess, although surprised by her father's speech, politely asked Manikin to accept her cloak. He loved her so much that his hands quivered when he felt the fur between his fingers.

"Princess, no gift on earth could please me more," he said. Then he left the Court to prepare for his journey to the Ice Mountain.

He had made his plans some time ago. Of the two thousand spaniels that had routed the army of Brandatimor, Manikin had brought back fifty to Trelintin. Keeping two as marching companions, he sent forty-eight ahead of him as scouts. The faithful Mousta, of course, begged for the privilege of accompanying his master.

Manikin refused his request. "You must stay with Sabella, Mousta. Farewell, my dear friend!"

He had decided to travel lightly. He took Sabella's cloak, his spear and bow, a little bundle of twigs, and a bag containing the magic dust that he'd swept up from the deck of the enchanted boat. Mounting his horse, he rode out from Trelintin with his two spaniels.

In this northern part of the kingdom the snows still lingered. The towns were winterbound. Wherever Manikin passed, the people gathered in the icy streets to demonstrate their love for the hero who'd saved them from Brandatimor's sword. Day by day the snows deepened. At the last little village Manikin caught up with the forty-eight spaniels who had preceded him. They crowded around the Prince wagging their tails and offering their paws. At this northernmost village Manikin parted with his horse. The last march would be on foot.

White and ghostly, the snows spread in every direction as

far as his eye could see. He felt as if he'd entered some strange and terrible country empty of all human beings. There were no roads, no trails, only a faint track that soon was lost. The polestar was his only guide.

"We will rest here," Manikin told his panting spaniels when he saw how exhausted they were from trudging through the deep snows. They wagged their tails as if to say: *You too must rest!*

Fifty pairs of eyes watched Manikin open his bundle of twigs and stick two or three of them into the snow. He sprinkled them with a pinch of his magic dust. Instantly the twigs began to sprout, thickening as they leaped upward, branching and blossoming. In a marvelously short time the camp was surrounded by groves of trees heavy with ripe fruit. They picked the fruit and built fires with the wood to warm themselves.

Manikin now dispatched a half dozen spaniels to reconnoiter their surroundings. Luck was with them. They found a horse loaded with bags of provisions trapped in a high drift. They helped the horse free itself and directed it to the remote little village far to the south. There it would find shelter and be fed. The spaniels dragged the provisions back to camp. When they saw that the bags were full of biscuits, they barked with joy. That night not a spaniel among them went to sleep hungry.

With morning, Manikin and his fifty spaniels left camp,

and again that night a few twigs sprinkled with the magic dust supplied wood for their fires and fruit for their supper. The spaniels would have preferred biscuits, but they had no choice. There came a day when they passed the frozen bodies of Manikin's many rivals. Rigid as icicles, they stood stiffly without sense or motion, as if spellbound by the Ice Mountain towering in the distance over a white world.

The weeks became months, and the Ice Mountain seemed to grow as they neared it. They shuddered at its unbelievable height and steep slopes. At night, huddled by their fires, man and dogs slept like the dead. At the beginning of the fourth month they reached the base of the huge mountain, and in the morning started the climb.

The cold was intense. Without their fires of magic wood, the blood in their veins would have frozen. Foot by foot they crawled up the slippery white slopes toward the Ice Palace at the very top.

With a wave of her wand the evil Fairy Gorgonzola had created the high walls, the battlements, the turrets and the white ghostly gates. "A royal Princess deserves a royal palace to house her heart," she had said with a wicked smile.

At last Manikin and his loyal spaniels ascended to the icy gates. Beyond them the heart of Sabella lay in deathly silence and icy sleep. Manikin stared at the huge white blocks of ice out of which the Ice Palace was built. He had never been so afraid of death. To keep alive they would have to make fires.

That was the danger! For the heat of the fires would melt the ice blocks and bring the whole vast structure tumbling down upon their heads!

The half-frozen climbers passed through the gates and entered a silent white hall. They hurried through endless white chambers until they stood at the foot of a vast throne. Numb with cold, his teeth chattering in his head, Manikin was compelled to start a small fire. As soon as he could bend his stiffened fingers, he rushed toward the throne. Upon the lowest step, carved in icy letters, were these words:

Whoever you are who by courage and virtue have won the heart of Sabella, enjoy peacefully the good fortune which you have earned.

He ran up the flight of gleaming white steps to the throne. There, on a cushion of snow, lay an enormous sparkling diamond which contained the heart of the lovely Princess Sabella. He had just enough strength left in his freezing body to seize the precious diamond before he fell unconscious upon the snowy cushion.

The spaniels bounded up the steps. Sinking their teeth into the icy folds of Manikin's clothing, they dragged him from the throne room.

It wasn't a minute too soon!

The still air cracked as if a thousand axes had begun to chop at the Fairy Palace. All around them they heard the

clang of the falling blocks. The white walls caved in and, slowly, the Ice Palace collapsed.

Not until the spaniels descended to the foot of the mountain did they pause to restore Manikin to consciousness. He opened his eyes and stared unbelievingly at the sparkling diamond clutched between his half-frozen fingers.

"The heart of Sabella!" he cried out in his joy.

The spaniels barked with happiness. It was as if they had said: *No man or woman is entirely human without a heart.*

With all speed Manikin and his loyal companions retraced their steps. When they passed the frozen bodies of his unsuccessful rivals, Manikin looked at them with pity. He was so happy he wanted happiness for all men. He gave orders to restore the ice-bound statues to life. Fires were built that thawed out the many Princes and their retainers who had succumbed to the bitter cold.

"We will never forget your kindness, Manikin!" the grateful Princes said. "We will let the whole world know that we owe our lives to you!"

When they reached the little village where Manikin had left his horse, he was escorted by five hundred Princes and their innumerable knights, squires, and pages. He was so modest and considerate that they all followed him willingly.

The climate became warmer as they climbed down from the northern heights. The sunny fields were bare of snow. One morning Mousta was seen running toward the procession. The spaniel was the bearer of great news. A sudden and wonderful change had come over the Princess Sabella. She no longer was cold and indifferent but gentle and thoughtful; she could talk of nothing but Manikin, of the hardships he'd endured on her account, and of her anxiety for him.

Manikin, smiling like a child, asked Mousta to repeat Sabella's tender words. There was no need to write them out in human script. By now Manikin understood the difficult language of the dogs.

Soon afterward, a courier arrived from Trelintin. The King and Queen, he said, had just heard of Manikin's success and wished to congratulate him with all their hearts. There was an even warmer message from Sabella. Manikin smiled—it seemed that he was always smiling—and sent Mousta back to the Princess.

When Mousta arrived at the palace Sabella kissed and hugged her pet—for wasn't he her lover's present?

At last the triumphant procession entered the capital and marched to the royal palace. King Farda-Kinbras and Queen Birbantine embraced Manikin, declaring that they regarded him as their heir and the future husband of the Princess Sabella. He was then conducted to her chambers.

Sabella, who had always been so quick with words, was speechless. Tears dimmed her eyes as she held out her hand. Manikin kissed it, and Sabella for the first time in her life blushed.

Manikin threw himself to his knees and held out the splendid diamond he'd brought back from the Ice Palace. "Dear Sabella," he whispered, "this treasure is yours. None of the dangers I've undergone are enough to make me deserve it!"

"Dear Manikin," she answered with another blush, "if I take it, it is only that I may give it back to you, since truly it belongs to you already."

Just then the King and Queen came into the chambers and interrupted the lovers with a score of questions. Over and over again—they were so excited!—they asked: "And didn't you find it very cold, Manikin?"

He would hear this same question echoed by a thousand people.

The King had come to request Manikin and the Princess to follow him to the Council Chamber where he intended to present the conqueror of the Ice Mountain as his son-in-law and heir. As the assembled nobles arose from their chairs, Manikin asked permission to speak first. The King nodded, and Manikin in a low clear voice told his whole story.

"Yes," he said as he finished, "I am the son of a peasant. But I hope that I have proved that man must be judged by his deeds. A man is a man—"

Thunder rumbled, and the sky outside the Council Chamber darkened. A white bolt of lightning hurled through the windows, and suddenly, robed in white, the good Fairy Genesta stood before them. Turning toward Manikin she said: "You have shown not only courage but a good heart. I am satisfied with you, very satisfied!"

She then revealed all that had happened at Manikin's christening, and told how his father the foolish King and his mother the foolish Queen had provoked the fury of a Fairy who could have been a sister of the evil Gorgonzola.

"Sabella's heart was stolen," she said, "as you all know. The Prince Manikin was robbed of his natural height and would have suffered other injuries if I hadn't brought him to my castle. There I gave him the education necessary for a man destined to command others." She smiled at Manikin and continued: "Your good heart has won you faithful friends. Very soon King Bayard and his subjects will regain their natural forms, and well do they merit it who have proved their loyalty to you."

Just then a Fairy chariot drawn by eagles flew into the Council Chamber. The foolish King and his foolish Queen stepped out and hurried to embrace their long-lost son. He was wearing Sabella's fine fur mantle, and suddenly his parents exclaimed with one voice: "He is all covered with fur!"

The meaning of the Fairy Genesta's mysterious words was now plain and clear: *You will not see your son again until he is all covered with fur. . . .*

Manikin's father and mother laughed and wept and laughed again. They caressed Sabella and wrung her hands—a favorite form of endearment with foolish people—while still other chariots could be seen approaching from all points of the compass.

"Your Majesty," the Fairy Genesta said to King Farda-Kinbras. "To celebrate this happy occasion I've taken the liberty of appointing your Court as a meeting place for all the Fairies who could spare the time to attend. I hope you can arrange the great ball which we have once every hundred years."

The King and the Fairy Genesta opened the ball together. Among the guests were King Bayard, restored to his natural form as a fine handsome man—as were all his subjects—and the Queen of the Spice Islands. Their wedding took place at the same time as that of Prince Manikin and Princess Sabella.

All lived happily ever after.

Prince Manikin, out of grateful remembrance of Sabella's first gift to him, gave her lovely name to the most beautiful of the martens. And that is why they are called *sables* to this day.

A NOTE

THE AUTHOR

Anne Claude Phillippe de Tubières, Comte de Caylus (1692-1765), was a scholar, an archaeologist, and a member of the Royal Academy who lived in France during the reigns of Louis XIV and Louis XV. As a man of letters, his mind reached out in all directions. He wrote about the great painters of the eighteenth century and about the antiquities of classical civilization; he wrote romances and compared old fairy tales to those of his time; and most important to us, he wrote his own fairy tales

THE ADAPTOR

Benjamin Appel has had a rich and varied literary career. Since the publication of his first book, Brain Guy *in 1934, he has written fifteen other novels, most recently* Hell's Kitchen *and* The Devil and W. Kaspar, *several non-fiction books including* The People Talk, *and numerous short stories. He was born in New York City and now lives in Roosevelt, New Jersey.*

THE ILLUSTRATOR

James K. Lambert is an artist and book designer. He was born in Parsons, West Virginia and now lives in New York City's Greenwich Village where he spends hours at his drawing board working on his exquisite drawings. He has illustrated several other books, including Gold Steps, Stone Steps, *a fairy tale, and* The Brothers Lionheart, *a legend.*